ABOUT THE AUTHOR

Christopher Pike was born in New York, but grew up in Los Angeles, where he still lives. Prior to becoming a writer he worked in a factory, painted houses and programmed computers. His hobbies include astronomy, meditating, running and making sure his books are prominently displayed in his local bookshop. As well as being a best-selling children's writer, he is also the author of three adult novels.

Spooksville

Spooksville

THE WISHING STONE

Christopher Pike

Hodder
Children's
Books

a division of Hodder Headline plc

Copyright © 1996 Christopher Pike

First published in the USA in 1995
by Pocket Books

First published in Great Britain in 1996
by Hodder Children's Books

The right of Christopher Pike to be identified as the Author of
the Work has been asserted by him in accordance with the
Copyright, Designs and Patents Act 1988.

10 9 8 7 6 5 4 3 2 1

A Catalogue record for this book is available from the British Library

ISBN 0 340 66121 6

Typeset by Avon Dataset Ltd, Bidford-on-Avon, Warks

Printed and bound in Great Britain by
Cox & Wyman Ltd, Reading, Berks.

Hodder Children's Books
a division of Hodder Headline plc
338 Euston Road
London NW1 3BH

One

Sally Wilcox saw the Wishing Stone first. For that reason she felt it belonged mainly to her. That was probably the same reason she suffered more than the others from the stone. The more you asked of it, the more it demanded in return. Of course, none of them knew that at first. But even if Sally had known, she probably would have made the same wishes all over again. She was a strong-willed girl, and rather impulsive.

They were not far from Spooksville, their home town, when they came upon the stone. Since dealing with Pan's leprechauns and fairies in the thick forest high in the hills overlooking the town, they had been staying closer to Spooksville, not wandering too deep into the dangerous places that were difficult to get out of. However, no place in or around Spooksville was really safe. The gang was only hiking in the foothills of the foothills when Sally stopped them and pointed toward the sparkle in the trees, some way off their path.

'What's that?' she asked, brushing aside her dark fringe.

'I don't see anything,' Adam Freeman said.

'Neither do I,' Watch said, removing his thick glasses and cleaning them on his shirtsleeve. 'Did you see an animal?'

'No,' Sally said, thoughtful. 'It was just a flash of light.'

'It could just have been a reflection,' Cindy Makey said, standing behind them.

'Obviously,' said Sally, who had been leading the group. 'But a reflection of what?' She paused. 'I think we should take a look.'

'I don't know,' Cindy said, fingering her long blonde hair. 'If we go off the path we'll get our clothes all dirty.'

'And we might run into a strange animal and have our internal organs ripped from our bodies,' Watch added.

Sally frowned at Watch. 'And you used to be so adventurous,' she said.

2

'I was younger then,' Watch said.

'You're only twelve now,' Adam observed. He nodded to Sally. 'I'll go with you and check it out. It shouldn't take long to hike over there.' Sally had pointed to the far side of the gully they were now hiking through.

'We should probably all go together,' Cindy said. 'It's not safe to separate out here.'

'It's not safe to be alive out here,' Sally said.

'But it is better than being dead,' Watch said.

They hiked in the direction of the supposed flash Sally had seen. When they reached the spot, they searched the area without finding anything unusual.

'It was probably just a trick of the light,' Adam said.

'Perhaps some debris from a crashed flying saucer,' Watch added.

But Sally was unconvinced. 'It was a bright flash. There must be something strange out here.'

'But strange is not necessarily good,' Cindy said.

Sally looked at her. 'Are you getting scared again?'

'Yes,' Cindy said sarcastically. 'Just being out in this wilderness with you makes me tremble in my shoes.'

3

'Let's continue our hike,' said Adam. 'Then we can go and get some ice cream.'

But Sally was unconvinced. 'I want to search the area one more time. I can do it myself. You guys rest here if you're tired.'

In fact, they were all sort of tired. The summer was nearly over, but the sun didn't know that. It was another hot, cloudless day. Adam, Cindy, and Watch plopped down on several boulders in the shade while Sally went off on her own. Cindy had brought a bottle of apple raspberry juice, and passed it around.

'Another ten days and school starts,' Watch said, taking a deep gulp of the juice and letting out a satisfied sigh. 'We won't have many more days like this.'

'We'll have the weekends free,' Adam said. 'We'll have plenty of time to hang out together and have fun.'

Watch shook his head as he passed the juice to Adam. 'You don't know the teachers in this town. They give you so much homework, you have to work on it all weekend just to keep up.'

'Why do they do that?' Cindy said. 'We don't all want to be rocket scientists when we grow up.'

'They just want to give us a chance to complete our studies,' Watch said.

'But what's the hurry?' Adam asked.

Watch shrugged. 'You've been here long enough to know the answer to that. Not that many kids who move here live long enough to graduate. Last year's junior high class graduated only a dozen people, and half of them were missing body parts.'

'What about the other half?' Adam asked reluctantly.

'Most of them were insane,' Watch said.

Cindy grimaced. 'That's horrible!'

'I don't know,' Watch said. 'They had a great all-night leaving party.'

'I hope we get to be in a lot of classes together,' Adam said.

Watch shook his head. 'It might be better to separate. Then, if there is an explosion or something in one of the classes, at least some of us will survive.'

'You have explosions at school?' Cindy asked. 'I don't believe it.'

'We had half a dozen explosions last year. Most of them were in chemistry class. The teacher used to work for the CIA.' Watch added, 'But I think they got rid of him.'

Suddenly they heard Sally shouting.

'I've found something! I've found something!'

Two

Sally had indeed found an extraordinary object. Nestled between two thick trees and sitting atop a granite boulder was a perfectly-sculpted black hand. It rose right out of the rock, its palm pointed upward toward the sky. Yet the fingers were not completely open; rather, they were slightly clenched around a cube-shaped crystal stone. This crystal was as big as a normal man's hand could comfortably hold, at most five centimetres on each side. Although the nearby trees stood close, a flicker of sunlight occasionally pierced their branches and the stone itself. When this happened there was a bright flash. The stone was clear but it also acted like a mirror, which puzzled Adam.

Now they knew what had caught Sally's eye.

'Isn't it beautiful?' Sally asked, excited.

'Yes,' said Cindy. 'But what is it?'

Adam nodded seriously. 'Good question. And where did it come from? I wonder.' He paused. 'Have you touched it yet, Sally?'

'No. I was waiting for you guys.'

'We might want to leave it alone,' Watch suggested. 'We don't know who it belongs to.'

'It belongs to me,' Sally said. 'I found it.'

'And does every bike you pass on the street belong to you?' Cindy asked. 'Every skateboard? Just because you found something doesn't mean it's yours.'

'It does if you find it in the middle of nowhere,' Sally said, reaching out her hand to pick up the crystal. Adam stopped her.

'Watch is right,' he said. 'We have to be careful.'

Sally was impatient. 'All right, say we take the safe course and talk about this thing for the next hour. In the end we all know that none of us is going to just leave it here for someone else to find. It's too pretty to just leave behind. I say we take it now and be done with it.'

'Hold on.' Adam peered at the black hand, trying to figure out what it was made of. It seemed to be some type of shiny metal, yet when he touched it, the hand felt warm. He told the others.

'Could it be alive?' Cindy whispered.

'It's black,' Watch said. 'If the sun was shining on it that might have made it hot.'

Adam studied the thick overhead trees. 'I don't think the sun made it warm.'

'I don't care about the hand,' Sally said. 'I'm only interested in the crystal.' Again she reached out to take it. 'Don't stop me, Adam.'

None of them stopped her this time, and a second later she was holding the clear cube, rubbing it with her fingers, savouring it as if it was a huge diamond.

'Maybe it is a diamond,' Sally said. 'Maybe I can sell it for ten million dollars.'

'Naturally you would share the profits with us, your best friends,' Cindy said.

Sally snorted. 'You wanted to leave it here. And now that I am holding it and you can see it's safe, you want to make money from it.'

'We reserve judgment at this time as to how safe it is,' Watch said.

'I'm more concerned with who it belongs to,' Adam said. 'I really wish you wouldn't take it, Sally.'

She remained stubborn. 'If anyone reports it missing I will be the first to return it.' She held it up to the sunlight and the crystal sparkled, sending tiny shafts of light into the trees. 'Until then it is mine.'

'Look!' Cindy cried. 'The black hand closed!'

Cindy was right. The palm that had once lightly grasped the crystal was now entirely shut. Apparently the fingers had folded over while they were talking.

'It is alive,' Cindy gasped. 'Quick, Sally, put the crystal back.'

Sally hesitated. 'Just because it moved doesn't mean it's alive.'

'I don't see many of these rocks getting up and doing a dance,' Watch said.

Adam spoke seriously. 'It doesn't belong to you, Sally. To take it is stealing.'

Sally considered. 'All right, I will put it back.' Carefully she held it close to the black hand, thinking it would reach up and grab it. When that didn't happen she tried to push it in between the clenched fingers. But the hand was tightly closed. Finally she gave up. 'It doesn't want it.'

'Then just leave it beside the hand,' Adam

suggested. 'It can reach over and grab it later, if it wants it.'

'No,' Sally said. 'I don't think that's fair. If it wants it, it should take it now.'

'I doubt disembodied black hands understand our concept of fairness,' Watch said.

'I'm not just going to leave it here,' Sally said.

'Thief,' Cindy muttered.

'Coward!' Sally snapped at her.

Adam held up his hands. 'Hold on, let's not have another fight. Maybe we can work out a compromise.'

'There is no compromise,' Sally said. 'I either take it or I don't take it.'

'You could leave a note with your home address on it,' Cindy said. 'That way if the black hand wants it back it can crawl to your house in the middle of the night, choke you to death, and take it back.'

'A novel suggestion,' Watch said.

'We can argue about this all day,' Adam said, resigned to Sally's wishes. 'If you're going to take it, then take it, and let's get out of here.'

'But please walk at least twenty metres behind us,' Cindy said.

'I always walk thirty metres in front of you.' Sally

11

clasped the crystal to her chest. 'I'm not afraid to go where no woman has gone before.'

They hiked back toward the path. Along the way Sally accidentally stubbed her toe and let out a groan. 'I wish I had a pair of new shoes,' she said, letting the others pass her on the path. 'These are so worn out – they're always hurting my feet.'

Then Sally let out a scream.

They turned anxiously. Sally was so stunned she couldn't even speak. She could only point down. Their eyes took a moment to register why she had screamed. Then it struck them and they let out their own sounds of amazement.

There were brand-new shoes on Sally's feet.

Three

'It must be a Wishing Stone,' Watch said a few minutes later, after they had all had a chance to catch their breaths. 'Bum has spoken about them before.'

'He has?' Sally asked, still amazed.

Watch nodded. 'He said they could be found on Earth during the Atlantis and Lemuria ages, tens of thousands of years ago. You remember he said that Spooksville was actually once a part of Lemuria. In fact, he says that Spooksville is all that is now left of Lemuria.'

'Did the people at that time make these Wishing Stones?' Adam asked.

Watch was thoughtful. 'Bum didn't go into too many details about them. But I got the impression the stones were put here by extraterrestrial visitors.'

'You mean aliens?' Cindy asked.

'Not necessarily,' Watch said. 'Bum believes this planet was originally colonised by humans from other planets.'

'He mentioned the Pleiades star cluster before,' Adam said. 'Did the Wishing Stones come from there?'

Watch was uncertain. 'He never said one way or the other, not clearly. But I got the impression they were from some place even farther away.'

'Did he say the stones were dangerous?' Cindy asked.

'He laughed when he talked about them, as he usually does when he talks about anything really mysterious,' Watch said. 'I was never sure if they were dangerous or not. But I do know that whoever holds one can ask for whatever he or she wants, and it will instantly appear.' He nodded to Sally's new sneakers. 'But we know that already.'

'Can I ask for as many wishes as I want?' Sally asked.

'I don't think the stones ever run out of power,' Watch said.

Sally squealed with delight. 'Wow! This is absolutely awesome. I'm going to have everything I ever wanted before I turn thirteen.'

'You can get *us* some things too,' Cindy said.

Sally laughed at her. '*Now* you change your mind. *Now* you think I did the right thing.'

Cindy was indignant. 'I just don't think you should be greedy.'

Sally patted her on the back. 'Don't worry, girl, you can have what you want. All I ask is that you be nice to me.'

Watch turned to Adam. 'I think the three of us had better accept what we already have.'

Sally smiled. 'That's not true, I can grant you guys a few wishes. But first I want to get a few things for myself.' She gestured for them to stand back. 'I don't want you crowding my presents.'

'Wait!' Adam said. 'We don't know what these wishes might cost.'

Sally stared at him as if he was nuts. 'Why should they cost me anything? This is a Wishing Stone. It's not a debt collector.'

'But you don't get anything for free in this world,' Adam said.

'But this stone did not come from this world,' Sally said.

'She has a point there,' Watch said.

15

Adam was still worried. 'I think you should be happy with your new pair of shoes and leave it at that.'

Sally laughed again. 'You have to start thinking big, Mr Adam. You don't accept a pair of shoes and walk away when you have the whole world at your fingertips. Now quieten down and let me think what I want.'

'You should get some new clothes,' Cindy suggested.

'Maybe a new watch,' Watch said.

'Shh,' Sally said, closing her eyes and letting her smile grow larger. 'I have something. Yes, this is what I want.' She paused and then blurted out the next words. 'I wish I had a million dollars!'

A million dollars suddenly appeared.

They were one-dollar bills and there were hundreds of stacks, which literally mounted up in piles above their heads. Adam could hardly believe his eyes. Reaching out, he grabbed one of the stacks and studied it. The dollars seemed genuine. Sally squealed again with joy.

'I'm rich!' she said.

'You should have asked for one hundred dollar denominations,' Watch said. 'You're never going to be able to carry this stuff back to your house.'

'Even if you could,' Cindy said. 'You couldn't fit it in your house.'

Sally snickered. 'You're just jealous! I'm a millionaire and you're not.'

'Well maybe you could give us a loan,' Watch said.

'I want some new clothes,' Cindy said suddenly.

'Wait a second,' Adam said. But no one was listening.

'What kind do you want?' Sally asked Cindy.

Cindy rubbed her hands together in expectation. 'I would love a black leather jacket and some black leather boots. Then, I need some clothes for school. How about a sharp Ann Klein suit? Light yellow, with designer buttons and gold-cuffed sleeves.'

'You need this to go to school in Spooksville?' Watch asked.

Sally waved her hand. 'It doesn't matter. If she wants it, she wants it.' Sally closed her eyes, then spoke aloud and wished for exactly what Cindy had just said.

The clothes did not appear.

Sally opened her eyes and studied the stone. 'It can't be broken already. Watch?'

'It's possible Cindy has to make her own wishes,' he said. 'You don't really want these clothes, not the way you wanted the million dollars. Give Cindy the stone and we'll see.'

'I'm not giving her the stone,' Sally said quickly.

'I'll give it back,' Cindy said.

'How do I know you will?' Sally asked in a dangerous voice.

Cindy was insulted. 'When have I ever stolen anything of yours?'

'When have I ever had a Wishing Stone before?' Sally asked.

'This is getting ridiculous.' Adam interrupted. 'This stone is already causing problems. Let's put it back now.'

'There are a couple of things I would like,' Watch said.

Adam was stunned. 'But I thought you agreed with me?'

Watch smiled. 'I did until I saw the million dollars.'

'I will give Watch the stone first,' Sally said. 'As an experiment.'

'What's wrong with me?' Cindy complained.

'Nothing's wrong with you,' Sally said impa-

18

tiently. 'But I have known Watch longer than you. I know for a fact that he'll give me the stone back when I ask for it.' She went to hand the stone to Watch, and then stopped. 'You will give it back to me, won't you?'

Watch shrugged. 'Sure.'

'Swear on your very life,' Sally ordered.

'It's not good to swear,' Cindy said.

'I swear to whatever you want me to swear to,' Watch said.

'All right.' Sally reluctantly handed over the stone. 'Don't break it.'

Watch held the stone close to his heart and closed his eyes. For a moment he concentrated deeply. Then he spoke. 'I wish for a refractor telescope with clock drive and computer-assisted star finder.'

The telescope appeared just off the path.

'Cool,' Watch said.

'Let me try!' Cindy exclaimed.

'It's my turn,' Sally snapped. 'Watch, give me the stone back.'

'Just a moment,' Watch said, closing his eyes once more. 'I wish for a laser pistol.'

A black pistol-shaped device materialised at his feet.

Watch knelt and picked it up. He pointed it in the direction of a nearby rock and pulled the trigger. There was a flash of red light. The rock exploded into a thousand pieces. The gang jumped, except for Watch. He studied the weapon closer.

'It's interesting,' he muttered.

'It's very powerful,' Adam gasped.

'What I mean,' Watch continued, 'is that the Wishing Stone was able to materialise something that we don't even have on this planet. That's further proof that it must be from another world.'

'I am waiting,' Sally said with her hand outstretched.

'Just a second,' Watch said, closing his eyes once more. 'I wish for the finest portable force shield generator in the entire galaxy.'

A small black oval-shaped object appeared at his feet.

Watch knelt and picked this up as well. There was a series of buttons on the side and he experimented with them for a moment. Then he handed the laser pistol to Adam.

'I want you to shoot me,' he said.

Adam shook his head. 'No way. We don't know

if that force-field generator will protect you. What if it doesn't? You'll die.'

'I have set the laser pistol on stun,' Watch said.

'How do you know for sure?' Adam asked.

'Shoot Sally and see if it knocks her out,' Watch said.

Sally jumped back and held out her hands. 'Don't shoot me! Shoot Cindy!'

Cindy didn't look too happy about the suggestion. 'Don't shoot anybody!' she shouted.

'Shoot a tree then,' Watch said. 'It really is set to stun.'

'You can't stun a tree,' Sally said. 'They're already permanently stunned.'

Nevertheless, Adam turned and shot the nearest tree. Once again a red beam of light shot out, but it left no noticeable impression on the tree bark. Adam decided it was safe enough to fire at his friend.

'You sure you have the force field on?' he asked Watch, taking aim.

'Pretty sure,' Watch said. 'The force field must be invisible. But the worst that can happen is that it knocks me out.'

'You should give me the Wishing Stone first,'

Sally said, moving to retrieve the stone from him. But then she seemed to bump into an invisible wall. She bounced back in mid-stride. Adam and Cindy laughed.

'The force field is definitely working,' Cindy said. 'Watch, you should leave it on all the time.'

'That way Sally will never get the stone back,' Adam added.

'Don't worry,' Watch reassured Sally. 'You will have it back in a second. But stand back right now. Adam, fire away.'

Once more Adam took aim with the laser and fired. The red beam sprayed over a point about half a metre from Watch's body, but it did not touch him. Adam ceased fire and Watch turned off the force field. Adam handed the laser back to his friend. Watch admired the two instruments.

'I've always wanted gadgets like this,' Watch said.

Adam was happy for him, despite his continuing fears about the Wishing Stone. 'I'm sure they will come in handy living in this town,' he said. 'Especially if the Cold People or the demons come back.'

'Thank you very much,' Sally said, snatching the Wishing Stone from Watch's hands. 'You already have more than me, and I found it. Stand back all of you. It is Christmas time in Spooksville.'

'But what about my new clothes?' Cindy asked.

'You'll get those when I'm finished,' Sally said.

She then proceeded to order up new clothes for herself, a new bedroom set, a new TV and stereo, and another million dollars – in one hundred dollar denominations. But when Cindy finally got her hands on the Wishing Stone she didn't hold back: more clothes, a new bike, hundreds of CDs, boxes of books. Soon the path was littered with so much it would take a couple of large trucks to haul it all away. Adam said as much.

'Most of this is just going to go to waste out here,' he said. 'You should have at least made your wishes back in town.'

'We can bring the stuff back piece by piece,' Sally said, stuffing her pockets with one hundred dollar bills. 'That reminds me, Adam. What do you want?'

Adam shook his head. 'Nothing.'

Sally held out the Wishing Stone. 'Come on, don't try to be a moralist. At least get yourself some new clothes. You look like your mother dresses you.'

Adam was insulted. 'My mother does buy all my clothes.'

'There you go,' Cindy said, trying on a new sweater over her tee shirt.

Adam was even more insulted. 'You really think I dress like a nerd?'

'I didn't say the nerd word,' Cindy said quickly.

'But she was obviously thinking it,' Sally said, still holding out the stone for him to take. 'Improve your image, Adam, what can it hurt?'

'You might want to get yourself a laser pistol,' Watch said. 'We could play war games together.'

Adam reluctantly accepted the Wishing Stone. 'I'm not going to wish for anything for myself,' he said.

'But it only works if you really want what you're wishing for,' Cindy said.

'I can really want something and it doesn't have to be for myself,' Adam said. Holding the Wishing Stone tightly, he closed his eyes and said, with as much feeling as possible, 'I wish for galactic peace.'

Nothing happened, of course. Nothing that they could see. The others stared at him as if he had lost his mind.

'What good is a wish like that?' Sally asked.

Adam shrugged. 'It's something I would like. For everybody to live in peace.'

'Wasn't world peace big enough for you?' Watch asked.

'We've been talking about people on other planets,' Adam said. 'Why should I leave them out?'

'But get something for yourself,' Cindy said. 'A new skateboard at least.'

'Yeah,' said Watch. 'You're making the rest of us feel guilty.'

But Adam handed the Wishing Stone back to Sally. 'Maybe later,' he said. 'I don't feel like I need anything right now.'

For the time being that settled that discussion. They spent the next ten minutes trying to figure out how much they could carry back to town. Even though it was a warm day, Cindy had gone behind a bush and dressed herself in *two* new outfits at once. Sally seemed preoccupied mainly with carrying away as much cash as possible. And Watch quickly discovered he couldn't move his telescope very far, and ended up only taking the laser pistol and the portable force field generator with him. For his part, Adam helped Cindy with her new bike.

'Next I'm going to wish for a gold credit card,'

Sally said as she skipped in front of them with the Wishing Stone in her hand.

Four

They were ten minutes on the way home when a dark figure in a red robe appeared on the path in front of them. He was hooded; the shadow cast by his hood made his face a black well of mystery. But in the shadow two eyes glittered with wicked red light. He was tall and his arms were exceptionally long. He raised a hand as they stood stunned by his sudden appearance. It was only then that they realised his hands were identical to the one on the granite boulder where they had found the Wishing Stone.

'I am the Collector,' he said in a strangely mechanical voice. 'I am here to collect on your debt.'

'I was worried something like this would happen,' Adam muttered.

'This character surpasses the worst worry I had,' Sally whispered, fear in her voice. 'What are we going to do?'

'Maybe you could give him some of your cash,' Cindy said anxiously.

'I don't think this guy can be bought off,' Watch said.

'Let me try talking to him,' Adam said, taking a shaky step forward. He waved to the dark figure and cleared his throat. 'Hi, my name's Adam Freeman and these are my friends. What exactly is this debt you're talking about?'

The dark figure lowered his right hand and a metallic scroll appeared in it. He read from it in his peculiar steel voice. It did not sound as if he was a living creature at all, but something built in an alien laboratory.

'Sara Wilcox – ten thousand and sixty-four gratoms,' he said. 'Cynthia Makey – one thousand and eighty-two gratoms. Watch – nine hundred and forty-one gratoms. Adam Freeman – you owe . . .' The dark figure trailed off for a moment. 'Your debt has yet to be added up, but it looks as if it will be large.' He paused. 'These were all placed on the same order.'

'This is from the stuff we wished for with the Wishing Stone?' Adam asked.

'Yes. The debt is due immediately and must be paid in full.'

'We did not know that,' Adam said.

'It does not matter. I am the Collector. I am here to collect your debts. Now.'

'Ask if we can just give the stuff back,' Cindy suggested.

'Maybe not all of it back,' Sally muttered.

'Can we just pay off the debt by returning the goods?' Adam asked.

'There is no refund policy. Your debts are due immediately. Hand over the gratoms now.'

'But we don't have any gratoms,' Watch said. 'We don't even know what they are.'

The Collector moved his fingers and the metallic scroll vanished. In its place was a small spherical object lined with numerous glowing buttons and flashing lights. It seemed to hum as it sat in the Collector's hand, filling each of them with an ominous feeling.

'The debt must be paid immediately,' the Collector said in his robotic voice. 'If you cannot pay then each of you must work off the debt on a slave planet.'

Adam held up a hand. 'Now wait a second. This is not fair. This Wishing Stone was just sitting in the middle of nowhere. No instructions came with it. There wasn't even a warning label on the side. We can't be responsible for debts we had no idea we were getting into.'

'I am a Collector,' the dark figure repeated. 'I am here to collect your debts. I do not argue over how you accumulated these debts. And since you have made it clear that you have no gratoms to pay for these debts, you will now be transported to a slave planet where you will spend the rest of your lives working off these debts.' He fiddled with the controls on the sphere in his hands. 'Stand ready to be transported to Amacron 37.'

'Wait!' Adam pleaded. 'We're not ready to be transported anywhere. We need to talk about this some more.'

'We should at least be allowed to talk to a lawyer,' Sally said, stepping forward and pointing an angry finger at the Collector. 'You show up here and say you're a Collector and we have to pay you and everything. How do we know you're not a fake? You haven't even shown us ID. You haven't even . . .'

Sally was cut off in mid sentence.

There was a flash of green light. It came from the sphere.

And Sally was gone. Just gone.

'On no,' Cindy cried.

There was another flash of green light.

Then Cindy was gone.

'Get out of the way, Adam!' Watch shouted.

Adam wasn't even given a chance to think. He dived to the side of the path. This time there was a burst of red light. Adam felt for sure he was on his way to some forsaken slave world. But then the Collector collapsed on the path and the transporting sphere rolled lazily into the bushes. Out the corner of his eye Adam saw Watch lowering his laser pistol.

'I wish I was a faster draw,' Watch said.

Adam understood. They had lost the girls. Adam stood and brushed off his trousers. Together they stepped to where the Collector had fallen. He lay face down, covered in his hood. Watch reached down and felt for a pulse at the Collector's neck, then jerked his hand back.

'I think I killed him,' he whispered. 'But the laser was set to stun.'

Adam shook his hand. 'I don't think this guy

was ever alive. You heard his mechanical voice. He's a robot.'

Watch stood and nodded grimly. 'You're probably right. Maybe the stun was enough to destroy his positronic brain.' He pointed to the sphere that had rolled into the bushes. 'I wonder if we can figure how to use that.'

Adam picked it up. Although small, there must have been at least twenty controls on the object. 'It would take a genius to understand how to operate it.'

'I'm supposed to have a genius IQ,' Watch said. 'Give it to me.'

Adam handed it over. 'What is your IQ?'

'One hundred and sixty.'

'I'm impressed.'

'I try not to brag about it,' Watch said.

While Watch was examining the device Adam studied the places where Cindy and Sally had disappeared. There were no burn marks on the ground, nothing to show that they had been beamed away to another planet. Amacron 37 – it sounded awfully far from home to Adam. He was about to turn back to Watch when a flash of light in the nearby grass caught his eye.

Sally had dropped the Wishing Stone.

Adam brought it over to Watch. 'It must have fallen from her hand during the transportation process,' Adam said.

'We might want to order up a few more laser pistols before the Collector's pals come looking for him,' Watch said.

'I think that will just bring his pals quicker.' Adam gestured to the fallen Collector, who had yet to move an inch. 'I don't think we have all that much time. Have you been able to figure out how it works?'

'I know how to turn it on. I watched the Collector when he zapped Sally and Cindy. But that is not the same as knowing how to operate it.'

'Maybe we don't have to know everything. The settings should be the same as when the Collector zapped the girls. If we zap ourselves, we should go to the same place.'

Watch was doubtful. 'Maybe.'

'We have to give it a try.'

Watch hesitated. 'Do we want to do that? I mean, that slave labour planet didn't sound like a relaxing vacation spot.'

'We have no choice. If we don't save the girls, who will?'

'If we can't save the girls, who's going to save us?'

Adam was astounded. 'I can't believe you would leave the girls to suffer lives of torment and misery.'

'I didn't say that was my first choice. I was just reviewing all our options.'

'What other option do we have?' Adam asked.

'We could go home and pretend none of this ever happened.' Watch stopped and scratched his head. 'But I don't suppose we would be able to live with that decision.' He gestured Adam closer. 'Get right beside me. I'll try to zap us both at the same time. That might increase the odds we go to the same place.'

Adam pressed up against his side and stared at the mysterious sphere, which Watch held at arm's length. 'What if it beams us into deep space?' he asked.

'Then we will have a hard time catching our breath.'

'Should we bring the Wishing Stone with us?'

'Yes,' Watch said, his finger on the purple button. 'We might be wishing for a couple of space suits in the next ten seconds.'

'I knew you were going to say that,' Adam replied, stuffing the stone in his pocket.

Watch pushed the button and the Earth vanished.

Five

Amacron 37 was desolate and miserable. A desert planet with two yellow moons and a purple sun, the wind blew thin and dry fifteen hours a day, which was the length of Amacron 37's day. Yet the air was not particularly hot – just unsatisfying. The world was obviously old and burnt out – there was hardly enough oxygen to support life. When Sally and Cindy first materialised on the planet, they wondered if they would survive the night.

There was no transition for them. They were on the path with Adam and Watch – and the Collector – and the next moment they were being herded toward a desolate barracks by a couple of steel robots with electric sticks. When the sticks touched you, they gave you a sharp jolt. Yet the girls did not argue with the robots or put up a fight, although

37

Sally was given a shock once just for stumbling on the sand. The voltage was not excessively high, but the stick did hurt. Basically they were in too much confusion to do anything much except what they were told.

The inside of the barracks was dusty and dark. They were shown to a couple of hard bunks and told to rest until the morning shift. Apparently they had been transported at the end of the work day, although the tiny purple sun was still in the sky, along with the two tired moons. Glancing around the dim barracks, they could see that not all the inhabitants were humanoid. There were a couple of huge bear-like creatures and one who seemed to be a cross between a spider and an overgrown butterfly. Everyone else seemed to be resting. No one stood to greet them, other than the two steely robots. One of the robots gestured with its electric stick.

'You will be called to labour in five zomas,' it said.

'How long is a zoma in human hours?' Sally asked.

'Forty minutes,' the robot said, and turned away with his companion.

Sally and Cindy sat on their respective bunks. They had left home only minutes ago but they already had sand in their ears from the short walk outside. Both looked as miserable as they felt.

'I wonder where the boys are?' Sally said finally.

'Maybe they were transported to another planet,' Cindy said.

'The Collector implied that we were all going to Amacron 37.' Sally paused. 'Maybe they escaped somehow.'

'I doubt it. They were probably just transported to another part of this planet.'

Sally was thoughtful. 'Watch had the laser pistol. Maybe he blew the Collector away.'

'Even if he did, I don't think that's going to help us at all.'

Sally sighed. 'All that good stuff isn't any use here.'

Cindy agreed. 'You would have thought they would at least have let us bring it with us. It looks like we'll be paying for it for a long time.'

A soft voice spoke near them. 'You only get what you wished for after you finish paying off your debts.'

They looked over at the neighbouring bunk. A

girl who appeared to be their age, with a green face and white eyes, sat up on her bunk and studied them. Her hair was long and black, so curly it looked as if it would be longer than she was if you straightened it all out. Yet she was beautiful, even with a green face, even by human standards. Plus her voice was a thing of music, gentle and melodious.

'Who are you?' Sally asked.

'My name is Hironee. What are your names?'

'I'm Sally and this is Cindy.' Sally paused. 'Have you been here long?'

Hironee was grave. 'Half my life. I assume you are both from Earth?'

'Yeah,' Cindy said. 'You've heard of the place?'

'I had a friend who was from there. His name was Charles. It was he who taught me your language. Except for the local boss and the robots – who know every language in the galaxy – I am the only one on Amacron 37 who knows English.'

'But what happened to Charles?' Cindy asked.

Hironee spoke sadly. 'He had been here for five years and then one day he just couldn't take it any more. He tried to escape.' Hironee lowered her head. 'The robots caught him in the deep desert, and burned him to a crisp.'

'Has anyone ever escaped from here?' Sally asked.

Hironee glanced up. 'There are stories that a few have escaped, over the last ten thousand years. But no one has got away while I have been here. This particular camp is surrounded by an invisible force field. Even to get out into the deep desert, you have to disable to force field. Charles did that by making a bomb out of local chemicals in the soil. But then there is nowhere to go in the desert. Either the elements kill you or the robots find you and cut you down with their lasers.'

'What planet are you from?' Cindy asked.

Hironee brightened. 'My planet is named Zanath. It is very beautiful, littered with what you would call tropical islands. I was very happy there.' She added wistfully, 'I miss it very much.'

'Were you brought here by a Collector?' Sally asked.

'Yes. I accidentally found a Wishing Stone and made a few wishes on it before the Collector appeared and demanded I pay him five hundred and sixteen gratoms.'

'Exactly how long have you been here?' Sally asked.

41

'Four of your years.'

'How many gratoms have you worked off in that time?'

'Three gratoms,' Hironee said, when she laughed softly, although it was a sad laugh. 'It really doesn't matter what your debt is. You will never pay it off before you die. That's the way the Kasters set up the system.'

'That's what I suspected,' Sally said grimly.

'Who are the Kasters?' Cindy asked.

'They are the ones who construct the Wishing Stones. They seed them on planets all over the galaxy, and use them to ensnare slave labour. The more advanced civilisations are aware of them and never use the stones. But the Kasters are always finding fresh slaves to work for them. They are shady businessmen, a greedy race of reptiles with a ruthless reputation for cheating and extortion. They also construct the robots who run this slave planet and many others like it.'

'Are there any Kasters here?' Sally asked.

'One. His name is Teeh, and he is horrible. He is the one I told you about who also speaks English. You'll meet him tomorrow – he goes out of his way to harass new slaves.' Hironee lowered her voice.

'Don't ever anger him. He'll peel the skin off your body and eat it in front of you. I've seen him do it before.'

'Why don't the more advanced civilisations in the galaxy stop the Kasters from taking slaves?' Cindy asked.

'The Kasters are a powerful and feared race. They only take slaves from those who have become indebted to them. This is what you would call a loophole in the galactic law. It allows them to operate just outside the law. Plus a lot of races still buy Kaster goods. There is always a market from them and some races prefer to keep the market open. Here on this planet you will make Kaster lamps for the rest of your lives.' Hironee shrugged. 'They're pretty good lamps. They last longer than us.'

'We will not be remaining here for the rest of our lives,' Sally said flatly. 'We are going to escape. I don't care how long it takes but I will not stay here and make lamps for a bunch of slimy reptiles.'

Hironee cautioned Sally to lower her voice. She glanced around the barracks, her white eyes glittering in the dark.

'Be careful what you say. Teeh has spies

everywhere. We can talk about such matters during the work shift when not so many ears are so close. But I can tell you now that it is better, in the long run, to accept your situation and try to live with it. There is no real chance of escape. Remember what happened to Charles.'

Sally lowered her voice to a whisper. 'Cindy and I are from Spooksville. It's the roughest town on Earth. You may have heard about it from Charles. It's prepared us for places like this. I don't want to brag about our past, but let's just say we have been in worse fixes than this before.'

'We have?' Cindy said.

Sally continued as if she hadn't heard her. 'Cindy and I are intelligent and resourceful kids. We will never accept this situation.' Sally glanced out the barracks window at the setting purple sun. 'The Kasters are going to regret they ever brought us here.'

Six

Adam and Watch materialised underground in a huge rocky cavern. The place was far from empty but their sudden appearance didn't even cause a stir. There had to be a hundred different kinds of races milling about the cavern. It seemed to be a marketplace of sorts. There were creatures of every colour and shape – some looked more like monsters than intelligent beings, especially the insectile beings. Adam shuddered as a couple walked close by and stared at them with several hundred emotionless eyes.

'Those two look like they would like to have us for dinner,' Adam muttered.

'Yeah,' Watch said. 'I think we had better get off this platform. It's probably where people beam into this place.'

They headed into the corner of the cavern, in the direction of what looked like a food place. There were numerous tables set up and people were feasting on an exotic array of dishes. In between the tables squat robots with square heads took orders and delivered the meals.

'Do you think this is Amacron 37?' Adam asked.

'No,' Watch said without hesitation. 'This is not a slave planet. All these people look like they're out for a pleasant afternoon of shopping.'

'But why should the transporter send us to another planet?'

'You forget that the Collector dropped the sphere as he fell,' Watch explained, still holding the instrument in his right hand. He had tucked the laser in his belt, under his shirt. 'A button was probably pushed that moved the destination control to the next place on the list.'

'Makes sense. But maybe someone here can tell us how to set the sphere for the slave planet.'

'We might want to find out about the place before we go barging in,' Watch said, finally putting the sphere in his front pocket.

Adam nodded. 'Good idea.' He pointed to the

far corner. 'Let's sit at that table over there and act like we belong here.'

They were not seated long when one of the short robots with a square head approached and wanted to take their order. It looked like a box of metal on wheels, except for its mouth, which faintly resembled a human mouth with a serious case of braces. It nodded as it approached and then gestured with an aluminium-coloured arm for them to speak, probably to find out what planet they were from and what language they spoke. They worked this out because right after Adam and Watch said hello, it replied in a clear, mechanical voice:

'Earth. English.'

'That's correct,' Watch said. 'You speak English?'

'Fluently. What would you two sentient beings like to eat and drink?'

Adam glanced at Watch. 'We don't have any gratoms. We better not order anything.'

'There is no charge for these services,' the robot interrupted. 'What would you like to eat and drink?'

Watch removed his thick glasses and cleaned them on his shirt. 'What do you have?' he asked.

'To repeat verbally our complete menu in the English language would take a long time,' the robot said. 'But we do have a wide variety of Earth dishes. Perhaps you could order and I will tell you if we can meet your needs.'

Adam brightened. 'Could I have a turkey sandwich on white toast, with lettuce and tomato, no mayonnaise? And an order of French fries and a large Coke?'

'Certainly,' the robot said. He turned to Watch. 'And you, sir?'

'I would like a pepperoni pizza with a large Coke.'

'Is that all?'

'Bring us a bag of chocolate chip cookies as well,' Watch said.

The robot was agreeable. 'Your order will take ten earth minutes to prepare. But I can bring your drinks within two minutes.' The robot turned to leave.

'Excuse me,' Adam said. 'Just before you go. What planet is this?'

'This is not a planet, sir, but an asteroid. Its name is Globar 92.'

'Are we far from Amacron 37?' Watch asked.

'Yes. Two thousand seven hundred and eighteen point six light years.'

'Thank you,' Adam said. 'My friend and I will have ice with our Cokes.'

The robot left and Watch nodded seriously. 'I suspected we were on an asteroid. Notice that this whole place is underground?'

'Yeah. But at least it's nice how you don't have to pay for lunch.'

'We should wait until we get our food to see how nice it is.'

But Watch's concerns proved groundless. The food – when it arrived – was very good. The Cokes, in fact, tasted identical to Earth's, but the robot explained that they were popular even in this part of the galaxy. Adam wolfed down his sandwich. Fighting with mysterious forces always made him hungry.

It was while they were eating their cookies that the stranger arrived. One moment they were alone and the next he was standing beside their table.

'May I join you?' he asked. But those were not exactly the words that came from his mouth. He spoke another language, but a voice box clipped to his belt provided them with the translation. Indeed, he had two extra boxes with him, which he quickly offered to Adam and Watch. Apparently they were universal translators that were often employed in such places as Globar 92. Adam and Watch clipped them to their own belts.

'Sure,' Adam said, as the box translated his word into the visitor's language. 'You can sit down.'

'But before you do we would prefer you to tell us what you want,' Watch said.

Adam could see Watch's point. The guy would have stood out at a Hallowe'en party. He was ghastly thin and white as a bed-sheet. His features were human as far as shape and function were concerned, but his eyes were completely blue, as was his long robe. To top it off he was smoking a fat cigar, and he didn't have a trace of hair on his body. On the crown of his head he wore a square blue cap. He blew cigar smoke in Watch's direction as Watch's comment was translated by the box translators on their belts.

'My name is Fur,' he said. 'I am well known in these parts. Ask anybody about me, they'll give me a good recommendation.'

'What would they recommend you for?' Adam asked.

'I am a trader,' Fur said. 'I make deals, good deals. May I sit down?'

'Yes,' Adam said. 'I'm Adam and this is Watch.'

'Pleased to meet you both.'

'Why are you called Fur?' Watch asked. 'You look as if you don't have a hair on your body.'

Fur appeared displeased as he pulled up a chair. 'Is it the custom on your world to insult somebody because they are bald?' He stroked his shiny white head. 'When I get a little ahead, I plan to have a hair transplant.'

'Where are they going to transplant it from?' Watch asked. 'Your twin sister?'

'Fur,' Adam said quickly. 'My friend doesn't mean to be rude. We're just curious about what you want.' He added, 'We're strangers to these parts.'

'I can see that,' Fur said. 'I spotted you the moment you came in, and have been studying you since.' He paused. 'I know you're from Earth, and that you're young by that society's standards.'

'We're not that young,' Watch said.

Fur smiled and they saw that his teeth were blue as well. 'I am not bald and you are not young. Very well, we are off to a good start.' He leaned closer and lowered his voice. The translator softened as well – it was clearly capable of distinguishing different emotional tones. 'I couldn't help noticing

51

that you came in carrying a Kaster transporter.'

'We did?' Adam asked. 'I mean, yeah, so what? It's a good make.'

Fur's smile broadened. 'The Kaster do not sell their transporters, not willingly. I can only assume you obtained this one through – how should I put it – unusual means.'

Watch shrugged. 'I don't see what business that is of yours.'

Fur shrugged. 'I am not interested in how you got it. I just want to know if you want to sell it.'

'No,' Watch said.

'Don't you want to know what I would give you for it?' Fur asked.

'No,' Watch said.

Adam raised a hand. 'Just a second, Watch. Let's listen and see what's available.' He paused. 'What are you offering, Mr Fur?'

'Just call me Fur. I can offer you pretty much whatever you want.' He laughed out loud. 'You really should ask around about me. They'll tell you that there's nothing Fur can't get you, and quick.'

'Except perhaps a Kaster transporter,' Watch said.

Fur lost his smile. 'They are not easily available,

it is true. But come, name your price. I am willing to bargain.'

'Can you give us twenty thousand gratoms?' Watch asked.

Fur blinked. 'You can't be serious? I don't have that kind of wealth. There isn't a sentient being in this place who does. What's the matter? Do you owe a Kaster Collector a Wishing Stone debt?'

Adam hesitated. 'As a matter of fact we do.'

Fur nodded, taking it all in. 'And the Collector appeared and tried to collect the debt. And somehow you two destroyed the Collector and took its transporter. I see the whole picture now. Am I right?'

'You're close,' Adam admitted. 'Before we could take care of the Collector, it managed to transport two of our friends to Amacron 37.' He added, 'That's Sally and Cindy. I don't suppose you've heard of them?'

Fur was grave. 'I have not heard of them nor will they ever be heard from again. If they have gone to a Kaster slave planet, there is no escape for them. They are doomed to work like slaves for the remainder of their lives.'

'Sally always was a good worker,' Watch said,

trying to put a positive spin on the matter. But Adam was appalled.

'There must be some way to save them,' he said.

Fur shook his head. Apparently that was still 'no' in that part of the galaxy.

'The Kaster keep perfect records,' he explained. 'They never allow a debt to go unpaid. That is the cornerstone of their ruthless reputation. Even if you could somehow break into Amacron 37 – which would be next to impossible – they would still have a record of your friend's debts. They would hunt them down to the last corner of the galaxy and make them pay.'

'Where are these records kept?' Watch asked.

Fur had to think. 'In various places. For Amacron 37 I imagine the records are stored on Tallas 4. That's the Orion sector. But you don't want to go there.'

'Why not?' Adam asked.

Fur wrinkled his nose. 'They have lousy food.'

Adam and Watch looked at each other.

'Is there another reason we can't go to Tallas 4, beside the lousy food?' Adam asked.

'Lots of reasons,' Fur said. 'The place is a heavily-fortified moon. Get within half a light year of it and the Kaster will blow you out of the sky.' He paused. 'Why would you want to go there?'

'Isn't it obvious?' Adam asked. 'We want to erase the record of our friends debts.'

Fur snorted. 'That isn't going to happen.'

Adam spoke in a stern voice. 'If it doesn't happen you're not going to get our Kaster transporter.'

Once again Fur lost his smile. 'I can't take you to Tallas 4. Even my wonderful ship – the *Fruitfly* – doesn't have a force field capable of withstanding what they would hit us with.'

'But what if you had a Kaster force field surrounding your ship?' Watch asked.

Fur was instantly interested. 'You have such a device?'

'We have a portable force field generator,' Adam said quickly. 'We don't know if that can protect your ship.'

'If it's the one I'm thinking of it can protect a whole battleship.' Fur stuck out his white hand. 'Let me see it.'

Watch hesitated. 'How do we know you will give it back once we hand it over?'

'Because if I cheated you here, in front of all these

people, my reputation would be permanently ruined. Don't worry, Watch. I just want to check its serial number.'

Watch took out the oval-shaped generator and gave it to Fur, who studied it intently. Apparently the serial number was not something you read on the side of the object. But finally Fur's face brightened.

'You must have wished for the top of the line,' he exclaimed.

'Naturally,' Watch said.

Fur continued. 'The size of the field can be adjusted to accommodate the *Fruitfly*. The field can even be altered so that it makes my ship temporarily invisible. But that does not mean that we can simply break into Tallas 4 and erase all the Kaster records. To do that we would have to blow up their computers, and that would take heavy fire power.'

Watch pulled out the laser pistol. 'Would this help?'

Fur was not impressed. 'You didn't ask for the top of the line there. That's a beryllium laser. They're dependable but nothing special.'

'Why can't we just beam ourselves to Tallas 4

using the Kaster transporter?' Adam asked.

'Tallas 4 is shielded, as is Amacron 37. You cannot transport through a shield. You need to take a ship, and then the ship has to either sneak by the shield with a Kaster vessel, or else break through it directly.' Fur shook his head. 'Either way the chances of success are not good. Why don't I give you something else for the transporter and the force field generator? I'd like them both. How about I give you my own house? I own an asteroid in the Taurus quadrant. You have great views of the Milky Way there, and the home-owner association charges are reasonable.'

'Sounds like a workable deal,' Watch said.

'No,' Adam exclaimed. 'We have to rescue our friends. You either help us save them or there's no deal.'

Fur smiled thinly. 'If I help you, I will probably end up as dead as you will end up. That doesn't sound like a good deal to me.'

'It's the only deal we have to offer you,' Adam said. 'Take it or leave it.'

'Are you sure I couldn't interest you in a couple of Sirian pleasure robots? You can have them designed to your own specifications.'

'We are too young to have girlfriends,' Watch said.

'But Sally and Cindy are still very important to us,' Adam added. 'Even if they aren't real girlfriends.'

Fur considered. 'You would have to give me both the Kaster transporter and Kaster force field generator. I wouldn't take one item.'

'Fine,' Adam said. 'As long as you take us back to Earth after we wreck the Kaster records and rescue the girls.'

Fur frowned and puffed on his cigar. 'Are you sure you want to go back home? The food's lousy there as well.' He added, 'Except for your Cokes. I can drink six of those in a day.'

'Do we have a deal?' Adam asked.

Fur hesitated. 'We'll probably all die. I wasn't kidding.'

Adam stuck out his hand. 'Do we have a deal?'

Fur glanced around and then finally offered his hand. 'I have a feeling I'm going to regret this,' he said.

Seven

The work shift on Amacron 37 was hard. First they were treated to a breakfast of cold, soggy porridge, and then they were herded into a stark warehouse where the Kaster lamps were assembled. Sally and Cindy were handed a welding gun and dark goggles and told to get to work. A supervising robot stood not far away, its electric stick held ready to shock those who were slow on the job. Cindy held up her welding gun.

'I don't know how to use this,' she said.

'We better figure out quick or scrap metal over there is going to light us up like a Christmas tree,' Sally said.

Fortunately Hironee appeared right then. The way she carried her welding gun, she looked like an expert. 'They have put you on the easy duty,' she explained, pointing to the half-finished lamps in front of them. They were big by human standards, made of very dark metal, very unattractive. 'You just have to weld the lower four joints into place. A child can do it.'

'That's good because we are only kids,' Cindy said, feeling anxious.

Hironee turned and spoke to the closest robot. 'I am going to show the humans how to perform their duties efficiently. Is that acceptable?'

'Efficient work is always acceptable,' the robot replied.

'You just have to know how to talk to a robot,' Hironee said, striking up the arc on her welding gun and pulling her dark goggles over her eyes. She bent down over the lamp in front of Sally. 'You have to make sure that the joint is firmly welded before you go on to the next one. Watch.'

While Hironee worked, the girls stood at her back and spoke in low tones. Sally did most of the talking.

'How many robots are there in this particular camp?' she asked.

'Twenty,' Hironee replied, the sparks of the welding gun spraying not far from her green face.

'And there's Teeh, who watches over them and us.'

'The reptilian Kaster?' Sally asked.

'Yes. He's worse than a dozen robots put together.'

'Do the robots have separate brains?' Sally asked. 'Or are they all controlled from a central place?'

'Both,' Hironee said. 'They have individual positronic brains, but they can be shut down from the computer in Teeh's office. But don't even dream of getting in there. It's heavily guarded.'

'Is the force field that surrounds this camp controlled from there?' Sally asked.

'Yes.'

'Did Charles bomb Teeh's office? Is that how he got through the force field?'

Hironee glanced behind them at the watching robot. 'No. He bombed the field generator itself. If he had been able to bomb the office, the robots wouldn't have caught him so quick and killed him. The computers would have crashed and the robots would have been disabled. But you must stop this line of thinking. I told you, no one can even get close to Teeh's office.'

Sally turned to Cindy. 'We have to get in there. We have to disable the computer. It's the only way.'

'But Hironee says that's impossible,' Cindy protested.

'Do you want to stay here?' Sally demanded.

'No,' Cindy said. 'But I don't want to die either. Besides, even if we are able to flee into the desert, what are we going to do out there?'

'Adam and Watch will come for us,' Sally said simply.

Cindy shook her head. 'You're dreaming. They're on another part of the planet. Their situation is as lousy as ours.'

'Hironee,' Sally said. 'If friends of ours were being sent here at the same time as us, would they have come here?'

'Were their wishes all placed on the same order?'

'Yes,' Sally said. 'The Collector specified that.'

'The they probably would have come here. But . . .' Hironee hesitated.

'What?' Cindy asked.

'If they resisted transportation they might have been killed back on Earth.'

Cindy's lower lip quivered. 'Oh no. That's probably what happened.'

'Nonsense,' Sally said impatiently. 'A single Collector could not take out Adam and Watch. I'm sure Watch was able to shoot him with his laser. Then they probably took the transporter device. I bet they're on their way here now.'

Hironee stopped welding and glanced up. 'I told you, this place is shielded. They couldn't transport here. They would have come in on a ship, a powerful ship.'

'But if we escape from this camp,' Sally said, 'they would be able to pick us up in the desert?'

'*If* you can escape here,' Hironee said. '*If* they are coming to your rescue. But those are two big ifs. You can't risk your life on them.'

'I would rather die than be a slave for the rest of my life,' Sally said.

Hironee cautioned them to be silent. 'Teeh is coming,' she said.

The Kaster boss was as ugly as his reputation. He looked like a crocodile that had one day decided to stand up on his hind legs. His thick tail flapped all over the place as he strode into the warehouse. He had a long snout and large dripping teeth. He wore silver-coloured armoured plate over his chest. But the worst thing were the sunglasses he sported at the end of his snout. For some reason they disturbed the girls more than anything else, possibly because they were cheap sunglasses. He waddled over to where they stood.

'Are you the new slaves?' he asked in a slobbery voice.

'Yes, sir,' Cindy said, standing stiffly, worried about having her skin peeled off and eaten in front of her.

'We are Sally and Cindy,' Sally said. 'I am Sally.'

'I am Cindy,' Cindy said.

'How come you're not working?' he demanded.

'I was just showing them how to use the welding gun, sir,' Hironee said.

Teeh was annoyed. 'Did I ask you? Was I talking to you?'

'No sir,' Hironee said, lowering her head.

'We just got here,' Sally said.

'I know that,' Teeh said. 'Do you think I'm blind? I know everybody here.' He leaned closer and studied Sally. 'Where are the other two?'

'Which other two?' Cindy asked.

'Your two friends,' Teeh said. 'Adam Freeman and Watch. They made wishes as well. I sent the Collector to fetch all four of you. Where are they?'

Cindy shrugged. 'We don't know.'

'I know,' Sally said suddenly.

'Where?' Teeh asked, losing his patience.

Sally looked around as if they were being spied on. 'I can't tell you here. We'd better talk in your office.' She added, 'It's a long story and the information could put your position in danger.'

Teeh frowned, as best a standing crocodile can. 'How can I be in danger?'

Sally leaned closer and spoke in his ear. 'Only I can tell you. I am here to help you.'

'Why should you, a human, help me?'

'Because I want to get ahead here,' Sally said. 'I don't mind stabbing my own people in the back.'

Teeh stepped back and looked around as well. She had sized him up correctly; he was very paranoid, and yet understood greedy ambition.

'Come with me to my office,' he ordered and turned away.

Hironee looked at Sally with worried eyes as she was led away. 'Be careful, Sally.'

'I know what I'm doing,' Sally whispered in reply. But she looked scared.

Eight

They were in deep space, a few hours away from Globar 92, with so many stars around that Adam felt as if he fallen into an alien's dream. The *Fruitfly* was not a large ship - the control room was no bigger than Adam's bedroom. The ceiling of the control room was clear as glass, as was the large viewing screen that Fur sat before. When Fur dimmed the lights it was easy to believe they were floating free in space without protective walls around them. Yet Adam found the sensation exhilarating, as he did Fur's explanation of how they would get to Tallas 4.

'We have to move there through a series of hyperjumps,' Fur said as Watch and Adam listened closely. 'Hyperspace is a region where the three dimensions of normal space can be folded in virtually no space. It makes interstellar travel possible. Without hyperjumps it would take centuries to journey between the stars.'

'Why do we have to make a series of jumps?' Watch asked. 'Why not just one huge jump?'

'That is theoretically possible,' Fur said. 'But in practice it is dangerous. Gravity affects each hyperjump. That's why we have moved away from Globar 92 for so long before making our first jump. We needed to get away from the sun that the asteroid circles. If we had tried to make a jump as soon as we left the asteroid, there would be no predicting where we would end up.'

'Could we have materialised inside a star?' Adam asked.

Fur smiled. 'It's possible, but unlikely. Most of space is extremely empty. Most probably we would have just ended up lost.'

'But each time you make a jump,' Watch said, 'you recalculate what your next jump will be based on the gravitational influences in the immediate area?'

'Exactly,' Fur said, reaching for his controls. 'Now get ready, we are about to make the first jump. You might feel a moment of disorientation.'

'I feel that way most of the time,' Watch muttered.

Fur pushed a button and the stars outside suddenly rushed toward them at a dizzy speed. Then they vanished, and there was a moment of utter blackness, so deep Adam wasn't even sure if he was still alive. Just as quickly, the stars returned, but now they were not nearly as bright. Fur explained that they were now closer to the edge of the galaxy, where the stars were not as dense.

'Tallas 4 is not far from here,' Fur said. 'The Kasters like to hide in places far from the beaten tracks. Still, we will have to make another two jumps to reach the moon.'

'Are they ugly creatures?' Adam asked seriously.

'Not as ugly as human beings, if that's what you mean,' Fur laughed. 'Ugly is a relative term. Why, when you first met me I bet you thought I was ugly.'

'No offence but I still do,' Watch said.

Fur stopped laughing. 'I'll have you know I have had many dates with women from your planet and most of them were happy to get to know me.'

'Where did you meet these women?' Adam asked.

'At Hallowe'en parties.'

'It figures,' Watch muttered.

'And you just invited them over to your spaceship?' Adam asked.

'Sure,' Fur said. 'I use that exact line. Works like a wonder.'

'Why do you call your ship the *Fruitfly*?' Watch asked. 'On Earth that would be considered a demeaning title.'

Fur was offended. 'On my home world fruit-flies are considered quite a delicacy.'

Adam was horrified. 'You mean you eat flies. Yuck!'

'They don't taste bad when you chase them down with a Coke,' Fur said, his skilful hands working the controls. 'Prepare for another jump. I am almost ready.'

Over the next thirty minutes they made two more quick hyperjumps. Finally the large, red, gaseous planet around which Tallas 4 orbited came into view. Yet they knew it was large only because Fur said it was. They were still so far from it that it looked smaller than the Moon as seen from Earth.

'But Tallas itself is ten times larger than your Jupiter,' Fur explained as he turned the ship toward the planet and switched on the gravity drive that powered it through normal space.

'How long will it take to get there?' Adam asked.

'Ten hours,' Fur said.

'We can't jump the remainder of the distance?' Watch asked.

'No, for two reasons,' Fur said. 'It is too short a distance and in either case the force field surrounding Tallas would cause us to explode when we attempted to exit hyperspace.'

'Have you installed the Kaster force field we lent you?' Watch asked.

'Yes, but I don't want to use it to get through the planet's force field,' Fur said. 'I don't know if it's strong enough, and the Kaster watch the perimeter of this system closely. What I prefer to do is attach my ship to a small asteroid that flies near the Tallas defence field. If we use the *Fruitfly*'s engines carefully, we should be able alter the orbit of the asteroid slightly and fly close to Tallas without setting off any alarms. This system is thick with asteroids and we'll just be another big rock flying by.'

'That's a clever scheme,' Watch said, impressed.

Fur smiled. 'Do you still think I'm so ugly, Watch?'

'You would look fine after getting a deep tan, a thick wig, and a pair of coloured contact lenses,' Watch said.

'But will we have to break free of the asteroid to get to the moon?' Adam asked.

'Yes,' Fur said. 'Only then will we turn on the force field, and make ourselves invisible. The force field draws a lot of energy – we can't keep it on too long.'

'How are we going to blow up their computers?' Watch asked.

'We're not going to blow them up,' fur said.

'But we have to erase those debt records,' Adam protested.

'There is no way we can use heavy fire power around this moon and not be destroyed,' Fur said. 'We would be spotted in a moment. My plan is to sneak onto the surface of the moon, find a terminal, and hopefully erase your friend's names from the computers. Kaster systems are always interlinked. Any terminal should give us access to all their records.'

'And I suppose we can wear lizard make-up so that no one notices us?' Watch said sarcastically.

Fur was offended. 'I have thought of that. Not

everyone who works on Tallas 4 is a Kaster. They have off-world help. That's what we'll be.'

'It sounds like a good plan to me,' Adam said, trying to be supportive.

Fur took a while to find a suitable asteroid, one that was heading the right way and one that was bumpy enough to hide their small ship. They actually set down on the backside of the asteroid, and for a long time they couldn't see the red planet Tallas or its four moons. But during that time Fur carefully applied the power of the ship's engines to the rear of the asteroid.

'This far out we only have to change its course slightly to cause it to fly inside the perimeter of the force field,' he explained.

'Could the force field destroy the asteroid?' Watch asked.

'The asteroid should be able to absorb the energy, and save us the shock. As soon as we're through, we'll race towards Tallas 4.'

Fur almost proved to be an optimist. Many hours later, as the asteroid finally began to contact the Kaster force field, their own ship began to shake violently. It felt as if the surface of the asteroid where they had anchored was ready to explode. A wave of shimmering blue energy glittered in the space all around them. Adam hung on to his seat for dear life.

'This is a rough ride!' he shouted over the noise.

Fur laughed heartily. 'This is nothing!'

The rollercoaster ride stopped a minute later. They were through the main force field. Yet they were still far from the moon, although for the first time they were able to see it; a dull orange-coloured globe that looked both cold and uninviting. Fur continued to work the controls.

'We are turning on our invisibility cloak now,' he said.

The view outside changed only slightly. It was as if a thin sheet of hazy material were placed over the starry sky, dulling it but not blocking it out. Fur fired the *Fruitfly*'s gravity engines and slowly they lifted off the asteroid. The feeling of slow motion may have been only an illusion. Quickly enough, the dull orange moon began to grow in size. Everything seemed to be going according to plan, when suddenly there was a massive explosion behind them. They did not hear it – because they were in the vacuum of space which does not transmit sound waves – but they saw it. The explosion was blinding.

74

'What was that?' Adam gasped.

Fur sounded worried. 'The asteroid. They fired on it.'

'But why shoot at a rock?' Watch asked.

'Probably because they thought someone was using it for the very purpose we just used it for,' Fur said. 'To get by the force field. If we hadn't taken off when we did we would be dead now.' He paused. 'I told you this was a risky mission.'

'Risk is our middle name,' Adam said proudly.

'I don't have a middle name,' Watch said. 'I can hardly remember my last name.'

'They will be alert now,' Fur said. 'Our only hope is that they assume we perished in the explosion.'

'How come they can't penetrate their own cloaking device?' Watch asked.

'They can if they know where to look,' Fur said. 'But they will probably not look for anyone trying to land on Tallas 4.'

'Why not?' Adam said. 'Because of the food?'

'Because no one would be that stupid,' Fur said grimly.

The orange moon continued to grow outside the viewscreen. Soon it dominated the sky, and Fur's hands were glued to the controls. He passed over what looked like a highly-advanced city, but shook his head when Watch asked if the computers could be located there.

'We will never find the computers themselves,' Fur said. 'They could be anywhere. We just need one terminal to tap in to.'

'Then why don't you just land anywhere?' Watch asked.

Obviously the tension was getting to Fur.

'Why don't you just sit quietly and let me do the flying, OK?' he snapped.

'I was just trying to make conversation,' Watch muttered.

Fur dropped down low a few minutes later. For a moment it seemed they would crash, he was coming in so swiftly. But at the last second he pulled up, and Adam felt his stomach go down to the floor. The orange terrain was now a blur. There were canyons, there were tall buildings. Moving so fast it was hard to tell one from the other. But just as quickly, Fur brought them to a halt in a dark place where they could see literally nothing.

'Where are we?' Adam gasped.

'In somebody's garage,' Fur said. 'I spotted it on

my instruments. They left it open and hopefully they're not home right now.'

'You mean, we just landed in somebody's house?' Watch asked.

'Why not?' Fur asked. 'All the houses here will have a terminal.' He stood up from his chair. 'Let's hurry, we won't have long before we're spotted.'

Of course the home Fur had chosen was not empty. Two irritated crocodile creatures rushed at them the moment they stepped inside the Kaster home. Watch had to draw his laser pistol and stun them. Yet the Kaster creatures continued to flap their tails even in unconsciousness. Fur stepped over them nonchalantly.

'You can say what you want about them,' Fur said. 'But they are neat housekeepers.'

The home was in fact gorgeous, filled with towering rooms, frequent waterfalls, dark pools. It seemed the Kasters liked to spend half their time in water, like crocodiles on Earth.

Fur found a computer terminal in what appeared to be a bedroom and sat down. He turned the machine on and slipped what looked like a high-tech floppy disk in a side panel. The computer screen and the keyboard were much larger and complex than similar human components. Fur explained as he worked.

'The software I have inserted into their system was written by a form of bacteria on Demavon 123. They are really smart bugs – everyone goes to them for the latest computer games. This program will trace back to the Kaster's main computers. The program is great at getting into supposedly impenetrable files.'

'We could use that kind of bacteria on Earth,' Watch said. 'Our computer games are getting boring.'

'They tried to visit your world once,' Fur said. 'But they just ended up giving a New York cabdriver a chest cold. He went to the doctor and got a shot of penicillin and that wiped out the whole Demavon 123 expedition.' Fur stopped and laughed. 'I bet the cab-driver didn't realise what kind of royalties he gave up with that one shot. The bugs could have taught him how to program his yellow cab to make hyperjumps.'

'It is upon such small and insignificant incidents that the destinies of worlds turn,' Watch observed.

Fur let out a sound of joy. 'I am in their records!

Quick, how do you spell Sally and Cindy's full names?'

'Sally is officially Sara Wilcox,' Adam said. 'That's Sara without an H. Cindy is Cynthia Makey. Do you need help with any of those spellings?'

'No,' Fur said, still excited. 'I'm calling up their records now. And in a few seconds I should be able to erase them from the system by putting in another Demavon 123 program designed for just such a purpose. Then we can be out of here and on our way to Amacron 37 with a clean slate for your friends in hand.'

'Both Adam and I actually have a little debt as well,' Watch said.

Fur nodded. 'I suspected as much. How do you spell your last name, Watch?'

'I don't think even the Kasters know that,' Adam muttered.

Five minutes later Fur was not so confident. He had put in the bacteria's other program and become ensnared in a complex web of information he couldn't extricate himself from. It was only after a few minutes of fighting with the computer that realisation struck and Fur leaped to his feet.

'They must be on to us,' he exclaimed. 'They are just feeding me this garbage to make me think I am getting closer to getting rid of the records. But it's hopeless, we have to get out of here.' He turned in the direction they had entered. Adam grabbed his arm, stopping him.

'But we have come so far,' Adam pleaded. 'We can't quit now.'

Fur brushed off his hand. 'Don't you see, Adam, they are tracking us this very moment, back to this terminal. If we don't get off this moon in the next few seconds we will all end up on a slave planet.' Fur suddenly stopped. There was a banging outside. 'What was that noise?'

'Sounded like a gang of Kaster police pounding on the front door,' Watch said.

Fur stuck out his hand. 'Give me your laser pistol.'

'What will you trade me in return?' Watch asked.

'Our lives,' Adam said. 'Just give it to him. What are you going to do, Fur?'

Fur grabbed the weapon from Watch and began to fiddle with the controls. 'This can be set to overload. When it does it makes a respectable blast.' He stalked toward the door to the bedroom. 'When you hear the explosion, run for the ship. Don't look left or right, just keep running.' Fur opened the door. 'It's time to show the Kaster cops what your human "trick or treat" means.'

Adam and Watch looked at each other.

'How do we get into situations like this?' Adam said.

'We keep poor company,' Watch replied.

'Sally?'

'Sally is dangerous,' Watch said. 'She's worse than the Kasters.'

'But she does make our lives more exciting.'

'That is true,' Watch agreed.

There was a massive explosion. It was so powerful, so deafening, that Adam and Watch were sure Fur had perished trying to stop the Kasters. But they remembered his last instruction, to run for his ship no matter what, and that's what they did. But they had to run through smoke and fire to get there. They were more than a little relieved to find Fur already at the controls of the *Fruitfly*.

'What happened?' Adam gasped.

Fur grinned. 'I answered the door and politely asked them what they wanted. They didn't even reply. They immediately opened fire.' He added, 'I didn't tell you guys that I had removed the force field generator and carried it into the house in my pocket. Their laser beams bounced back on them and caused their whole load of weapons to explode.'

'You carried the force field on your own body so that at least you would be safe,' Watch said.

'Hey,' Fur said. 'I'm the only one here who can fly this ship. That makes me the most valuable person. Anyway, I have hooked the generator back up to the ship.' Fur nodded at the mess outside the forward viewing screen. 'We're going to need it like we never needed it before. Especially in the next two minutes.'

'If we fly into orbit they'll just blow us out of the sky,' Adam said as Fur started the ship's engines. Fur's hands flew over the controls.

'We're not going to stay around long enough for them to take aim,' Fur said.

'You're going to hyperjump as soon as we're in space,' Watch said, excited at the prospect.

'Exactly,' Fur said. 'Hold on.'

'But you said such a jump is uncontrollable!' Adam shouted as he was pressed back into his seat by the force of the acceleration. They roared out of what was left of the Kaster garage. The haunting orange sky loomed above them. But very quickly it began to darken, as they ploughed beyond the atmosphere and into space.

'Better an uncontrollable jump than certain death!' Fur yelled back. He glanced above as they broke completely free of the atmosphere. Mixed in the stars, there were three Kaster warships already rushing towards them. 'Prepare to jump!'

'But we still need to get to Amacron 37!' Adam yelled. 'We have to rescue the girls!'

'We rescue ourselves first!' Fur yelled.

And with that they jumped into hyperspace.

With no idea where they would end up.

Nine

Sally stood in Teeh's office and wondered what she was supposed to tell the Kaster boss. So intent had she been on just getting to the head of the compound's power, she had not planned how she was going to get out of the office. Teeh, still slobbering and still wearing his cheap sunglasses, sat down opposite her. There was no other chair and he didn't offer to get her one. The crocodile boss put his scaly feet up on his dirty desk and looked at her as if she had better have a good reason for requesting a private audience.

'Well?' he said. 'Where are your friends?'

Sally swallowed. 'They're not here.'

'I know they're not here. Do I look stupid or what? Where are they?'

'They're on their way here,' she said.

'What are you talking about?'

'Has the Collector you sent to fetch us returned?'

'I ask the questions here!' Teeh paused. 'No. It hasn't.'

'Adam and Watch destroyed it.'

Teeh sat up straight. 'How do you know this?'

Sally felt herself getting in the mood to tell some really great lies.

It was a special feeling of wonderful power.

'I know them. They're powerful young men. At this very moment they have allied themselves with other powerful beings and they are on their way here to rescue Cindy and me.'

Teeh snorted. 'You're dreaming. No one tries to rescue anyone from Amacron 37. It's a dust-bowl – hardly anyone can find this place.'

'Then where is your Collector?' Sally asked.

Teeh scratched his scaly head. 'Well, I don't rightly know. I suppose it is possible your friends got the upper hand with him. What is it they ordered anyway?'

'Watch ordered a laser pistol and a personal force field generator.' Sally added, 'He also got himself a telescope.'

Teeh frowned. 'We have to stop offering those

86

personal force field generators. We lose more Collectors that way.' He paused and studied her. 'Why are you telling me all this?'

'I told you, I want to get ahead. And I don't mind betraying my friends to do it. I tell you seriously, they are on their way here this very minute. If you don't take care, they will remove you as boss of this slave planet.'

'Who are the powerful beings they have made friends with?'

Sally darkened her expression. 'The Treeboards.'

'I haven't heard of them. What sector are they from?'

'They don't even come from this galaxy. They're from a black hole at the edge of the universe. They're an ancient race. They were highly evolved when your race and mine were bacteria swimming in primeval mud. They have powers we can't even dream of.'

'Then what would they want with your friends?'

Sally spoke in wicked whispers. 'They have allied themselves with Adam and Watch because they have a common goal. You see, the Treeboards have an ancient and undying hatred for ugly lizards like . . . for reptilian super-races like your own.

Adam and Watch have stolen your Collector's transporter. Now they have an easy map that leads straight here, and the evil Treeboards want to come along for the ride, to destroy you when they see you. To destroy all Kasters, wherever they may be.' Sally paused for effect. 'The shield you have erected around Amacron 37 will not stop them. It won't even come close.'

Teeh appeared unsure of himself. 'This story sounds outlandish. Can you prove that these Treeboards even exist?'

'Yes. I spent time with them, on a lost moon circling a dead quasar, ten billion light years from here. They taught me many of their secrets, and I can show you some of those secrets now. I can teach you how to strengthen the force field that surrounds this planet so that even the Treeboards – even Watch and Adam – cannot get through it with their fleet of super tachyon spaceships.'

Teeh raised an eyebrow. 'What are those?'

'Highly-developed vessels that you'll never see in a Collector's Christmas catalogue. Listen to me, Teeh, please, I am the only one that can save you. If you will just give me a few minutes with your computer, I can prove it to you.'

Teeh considered. 'What do you want in return for this help?'

'You must erase my Wishing Stone debt.'

'What about the debt of your friend, Cindy?'

Sally waved her hand. 'She is of no concern to me. She can rot here for the rest of eternity for all I care.'

Teeh grinned. She had hit the right nerve. He was now convinced.

'Spoken like a true Kaster,' he said. 'Are you sure you don't have reptilian blood in your veins, Sally?'

'My grandmother always used to say my grandfather was a snake. I never met him myself but I heard the stories. He was your kind of man, Teeh. And I am your girl. Where's your computer?'

Teeh stood and moved toward an elaborate control panel. 'You understand while you work on my computer I have to stand and supervise?'

Sally stood and followed him to the computer. It looked like a bunch of lights and buttons to her. She wished Watch was with her now.

'Naturally,' she said. 'It is my hope that I can teach you a few things.' She added, 'I mean that with all due respect, of course.'

'Of course,' Teeh said, in a good mood, for him.

'You are familiar with my operating system? The famous Kaster double matrix algorithm TEC dot software?'

Sally waved her hand as she sat down in front of the massive computer. 'I learned about that when I was in first grade. It is an extremely primitive system when compared to what the Treeboards use.' Sally touched the keyboards and then paused. 'I need an electric stick.'

'What?'

'One of those sticks that your primitive robots carry. I need one.'

'What for?'

'I am going to link it into your computer system so that this whole planet will be transformed into one cosmic-sized electric stick which will be capable of repelling the super tachyon fleet that races toward this planet at this very instant.' Sally had to pause to catch her breath. 'Do you have one in your desk?'

Teeh turned back to his desk. 'I believe so. But frankly this kind of technology confuses me. I have never seen anything like it.'

'Neither have I,' whispered Sally.

'What?'

'Nothing. Everything will quickly become clear. The power of your protective shield will change beyond your wildest dreams. With this technology, you will be the single most power Kaster in this section of the galaxy.'

Teeh found an electric stick in one of his drawers. 'I have not had the advantage of your obviously extensive education. How long will it take me to comprehend the Treeboard technology?'

'A sly lizard like . . . I mean, a brilliant Kaster like you – you will know more than I do before we both leave this room.' She stuck out her hand and took the electric stick. 'Now I just need to know one other thing.'

Teeh stood nearby. 'What?'

'Where does this computer plug in?'

'What do you mean?'

'Its power source. Where does it draw its power from?'

Teeh nodded to a black box to the side of the control panel. 'From there. Do you need more power? I can have extra cables brought in.'

'Maybe. Open the power box. Let me study it.'

Teeh did so. It looked much like a fuse box back home.

Sally turned on the electric stick and got up. 'Stand aside, Teeh.'

He did as she requested but a flicker of doubt crossed his face.

'What are you doing?' he asked.

'Changing the polarity of the situation.' Sally rammed the tip of the electric stick into the black box. The thing literally exploded in sparks. She knew immediately that the damage was enough to knock out the force field and all the robots. She turned the stick on Teeh and smiled wickedly up at his blustering expression. 'I am changing everything,' she said.

He was enraged. 'You will pay for this!'

'Wrong! We're through paying!'

And with that Sally stuck the electric stick up his fat snout.

Tech turned a deeper green than normal and fainted.

Sally stepped on his cheap sunglasses as she fled the room.

Ten

They came out of hyperspace in the centre of the galaxy. There were so many stars in the sky that it was hard to find any black space. Fur quickly handed them each a pair of thick sunglasses. Watch stared out of the viewing screen, enthralled.

'I'll never see anything like this in my telescope,' he said.

'If we don't get out of here quickly we won't be seeing, period,' Fur said.

'Why not?' Adam asked.

'There are tremendous levels of radiation at the galactic core,' Fur explained. 'Our force field is keeping them at bay for the moment but that situation will not last. The first thing this kind of radiation burns is the optic nerves.'

'Can we make another hyperjump so close

to all these stars?' Watch asked.

Fur was grim. 'We have no choice. But it could tear us apart.'

'We will go out in a blaze of glory,' Watch said, still staring at the stars.

'What glory?' Adam asked. 'We failed in our quest. We weren't able to destroy the records on Tallas 4. Our debts will last for ever. We will never be free of them.'

'Isn't there a saying on your world?' Fur said as he worked the controls. 'It ain't over till it's over? That's my motto. Hold on, we're going to make another jump, and I can guarantee this one will be rough.'

They leaped into hyperspace, and this jump was different from the others. Not really rough, but it seemed as if the period of blackness lasted for ever. During the time Adam wondered if that was not literally the case, if they would not be trapped for eternity outside of normal space and time. But finally the stars reappeared. Fur checked his navigation computer.

'I know where we are!' he exclaimed.

'Where?' asked Adam.

'In the Beta quadrant. We're not far from

Amacron 37.' He paused. 'Are you sure you still want to go there? We'll never get through their force fields. Slave planets are strictly off limits.'

'We have to try,' Adam said.

'But we can always try later,' Watch said.

'Watch!' Adam complained. 'I'm disappointed in you.'

'I would rather live with your disappointment than die in a Kaster force field,' Watch replied. But then he paused and gave it some thought. 'But I suppose we might succeed in the end. We usually do.' He nodded to Fur. 'Plot a hyperjump for Amacron 37.'

'And may the Force be with us,' Adam said.

'*Star Wars*,' Fur quipped. 'Great movie.'

A few minutes later they were again flying through hyperspace.

When Sally ran from Teeh's office, she saw immediately that her plan had worked. The robot guards were all standing immobilised. Yet her plan had its limits, as Cindy had pointed out. There was no where to go except into the desert.

Cindy and Hironee came out of the work warehouse as Sally ran over. The other slaves were still inside, casting hesitant looks in their direction, but with nothing else to do now that the power was off all over the compound.

'What's happened?' Hironee asked.

'I disabled the computer,' Sally said. 'That means that the force field is down for the time being. We have to get out of here before it comes back on-line.'

'But what happened to Teeh?' Cindy asked.

'He's taking a nap,' Sally said.

'A nap?' Hironee said, puzzled.

'With an electric toothpick up his nose. Look, we can talk about this once we're deep in the desert and clear of the force field.'

Cindy nodded. 'I'll get us water bottles, a pack of supplies.' She dashed off to collect the stuff. For the moment Sally was left alone with Hironee, although a robot stood perfectly still nearby, caught in mid-stride by the drop in power. Sally was surprised to see Hironee was not excited and asked her what was the matter. The green-faced girl answered with her head down.

'We can't go into the desert,' she said softly. 'Charles went into the desert and he died.'

Sally put a hand on her shoulder. 'Charles did not knock out the robots like we have. They were the ones who hunted him down and killed him. Also, Charles was alone. In the desert we can help each other.' Sally paused. 'Something else is bothering you.'

Hironee nodded weakly. 'I hate this place. I've told you how much I hate it. But I've been here half my life. It's home to me now. I know that sounds silly but I'm afraid to leave it.' She stopped and there were tears in her eyes. 'You and Cindy had better leave without me.'

'Nonsense. We will never do that.' Sally gave her a hug and then gestured to the barren landscape. 'This is no home for a person like you. Try to remember what Zanath was like – the blue water, the green islands, the warm yellow sun in the clear sky. That's your home, Hironee, and if you come with us you might see it again soon. But I'm not promising you will. Maybe you will die in the desert like Charles. That's a definite possibility. But you have to know deep inside that it's better to die free than live as a slave.'

Hironee smiled at the words. 'You never told me, Sally, that you were such a motivational speaker.'

Sally laughed. 'My talents are endless.' She turned toward the building where Cindy had disappeared. 'Let's take what supplies we can carry and let's get out of here before Mr Lizard Breath wakes up.'

They came out of hyperspace much closer to Amacron 37 than they had been to the other worlds when they finished making their jumps. Fur explained that he had intentionally cut it close so that the Kasters would have less time to spot them.

'But we can circle around the planet until they shoot us down if we're hoping to get into their slave compounds,' he said gloomily as they raced toward the desert planet, a purple sun hanging in the sky off to their right.

'Are the force fields just around the slave compounds?' Watch asked.

'Usually,' Fur said. 'There's no point in protecting all of a planet like this. It's mostly dust and sand. The Kasters usually concentrate their energy where it's most needed. But that allows them to erect an even stronger force field in a small area. Don't fool yourself, this place is more protected than Tallas 4 was.'

'Where we were far from a huge success,' Watch observed.

'Is there no way to get through the force fields?' Adam asked, feeling frustrated.

'We can try,' Fur said. 'We can turn the generator Watch has lent me up to full power and try to smash through. But there is an excellent chance we will explode.'

'Better not risk it,' Watch said, having second thoughts.

'We have to give it a try,' Adam said.

Fur stared at him. 'These two girls must be pretty special.'

'One of them is,' Watch said. 'The other is just unusual.'

'They are our friends,' Adam said. 'That's what matters.'

Fur was wistful. 'I wish I had friends as loyal as you two.' He added, 'Or at least as loyal as you, Adam.' Something on the control panel caught his eye. He pushed a couple of buttons, seemingly rechecking his readings. 'This is odd.'

'What is it?' Adam asked.

'The southernmost compound on Amacron 37 – their force field is shut down. Not only that, but there are three life-signs heading away from the compound, heading deep into the desert.'

'It must be the girls!' Adam exclaimed.

'I thought there were only two of them,' Fur said.

'They make friends fast,' Watch said. 'At least Cindy does.'

Something else on the control panel caught Fur's eye. But rather than trying to ascertain exactly what his instruments were showing, he leaned his head back and stared up at the window on the ceiling of the control room. Adam and Watch did likewise, in time to see a fleet of warships materialise in normal space. Clearly the ships had just completed a jump through hyperspace. They were grey in colour, long and sleek, with red fins and smouldering weapon-ports.

'The Kaster,' Fur said softly, stunned. 'They must have followed us here from Tallas 4.'

'They could trace us through hyperspace?' Watched asked.

Fur shook his head. 'No. But they didn't have to. They figured we were coming here because we were trying to erase records related to Amacron 37.'

'Do we have to surrender?' Adam asked.

Fur was grim. 'The Kaster do not take prisoners in a situation like this.'

'Then we must try to jump into hyperspace again,' Watch said.

'No,' Adam said. 'We have to get the girls first.'

'If we land, we will be completely helpless,' Fur said. 'They will destroy us at their leisure. I agree with Watch. We must try to escape.' Fur went to push the button that would launch them into hyperspace. But Adam stopped him by putting a hand on his arm.

'The girls have knocked out the Amacron 37 force field when you said that was impossible,' Adam said. 'They are out in the desert, fighting for their lives, for freedom. How can we just abandon them when they have fought so hard and we are so close to them?'

Watch spoke up. 'Adam has a point. Even I would feel guilty leaving them at this point.'

Fur studied his instruments. 'They are not alone in the desert. A force of robots is now on their tail.' He looked at them. 'If we land we will have enemies on all sides.'

Adam didn't hesitate. 'Land. We either save them or else we all die together.'

Watch patted Fur on the back and tried to

reassure the trader. 'We're all from Spooksville. We have an excellent track record in hopeless situations.'

Fur sighed. 'I don't.'

Eleven

Hironee saw the *Fruitfly* first. They were trudging around a massive sand-dune when it appeared in the sky above them. Burning with the flames of re-entry, heading straight for them like a meteor shot out of a stellar cannon.

'Look!' Hironee shouted.

Sally and Cindy almost fell over when they saw the ship.

'Is it a Kaster vessel?' Sally asked, fully expecting the answer to be yes.

Hironee squinted. 'No, I don't think so. It looks more like a trader ship.'

Sally looked at Cindy. 'It could be Adam and Watch.'

Cindy nodded anxiously. 'Hope so.'

But just then all hope seemed to fade. The fleet

of Kaster warships – chasing the trader vessel – became visible at the same time that Teeh and his robots rounded the sand-dune behind the girls. The Kaster warships had torpedo tubes on both sides that glowed with a wicked red light. Teeh had a small fleet of powerful ground vehicles that resembled open-air tanks. Both Kaster groups seemed to be in the middle of taking aim. Yet perhaps Teeh, seeing the ships overhead, warned them off. The slimy boss probably didn't want to get blasted with the humans. Overhead the ships suddenly veered off to the side. Yet they did not fly away, rather they began to swoop in at a low altitude.

In the meantime the trader ship landed nearby.

Adam and Watch and a ghost character with a bald head and a cigar in his mouth jumped out. The girls ran to the boys and embraced them.

'Are we glad to see you!' Cindy exclaimed, giving Adam a big hug.

'We are happy to see you!' Adam said, hugging her back.

'I was the one who disabled the Kaster force field,' Sally said quickly.

'I was the one who blew up the Kaster house,'

Fur said, watching both the approaching land army and the hovering warships. 'But it looks like we both only managed to anger the wrong people.'

'And who may I ask are you?' Sally asked suspiciously.

Fur bowed. 'I am Fur and I am here to rescue you.' He glanced at Watch. 'This must be the unusual one.'

'I knew you would spot her immediately,' Watch said.

'I will have you know that it was I who said you were on your way here to rescue us,' Sally said. 'While Cindy here was ready to bury you, as usual I might add.'

Fur gestured to the approaching armoured car, which carried several robots and the grand master of slobbers himself – Kaster boss Teeh. His snout looked swollen and sore. He held a black laser rifle in his two stubby arms.

'I think we might all be buried in a few minutes,' Fur said.

Teeh parked only a few metres away and his robots immediately jumped from the armoured vehicle and surrounded them on all sides, pointing mean-looking lasers at their heads. Teeh likewise approached and he did not look in a good mood. Although he carried a weapon, his free hand kept moving to his bruised snout. He went straight to Sally and glared at her.

'I am going to peel you alive!' he swore. 'I will swallow your flesh before your very eyes! You will die with your own screams in your ears!'

Sally spoke sweetly. 'Did the Treeboards hurt your nose, Mr Teeh?'

Teeh growled. 'There are no Treeboards!'

'Of course there are,' Watch said. 'All boards come from trees.'

'I know that!' Teeh said. 'Do I look stupid or something? I . . .'

'You do look stupid,' Cindy interrupted, surprising them all. She just shrugged when they stared at her. 'He looks like a stupid crocodile from a dirty swamp. What can I say?'

Teeh was not amused. 'You will pay for that!'

Sally snorted. 'I told you, we're through paying. If you're going to kill us, kill us now and get it over with. We're not afraid to die.'

'I would like to mention that Sally does not speak for all of us,' Watch said.

'I would like to second that,' Fur said.

Just then one of the Kaster warships settled to the ground behind *Fruitfly*. The vessel was massive, powerful; it cast a steaming shadow over the entire area. An official-looking Kaster captain with a host of lizard guards approached, making a mess of the sand-dune with their swishing tails. The captain clearly outranked Teeh, who quickly bowed to the commander of the warship.

'Captain Thorath,' Teeh said. 'A pleasure. What brings you to Amacron 37?'

Captain Thorath pointed a scaly finger at Fur. 'This trader invaded Tallas 4 and tried to wipe out several debt records from our computer files. I am here to arrest him and bring him back to Tallas 4 for immediate trial and execution.'

'At least you get a trial,' Watch said to Fur.

'It sounds like I will have trouble finding an impartial jury,' Fur said.

'What about these other two humans?' Teeh asked Captain Thorath, pointing to Adam and Watch. Captain Thorath did not answer immediately. He seemed to be caught off guard by the question. He studied Adam and Watch, seemingly trying to figure out a problem that was bothering him.

'Which one of you is Adam?' he asked finally.

'I am,' Adam said.

'Tell him what a slob he is,' Sally said in his ear. 'Don't let him intimidate you.'

'Shh,' Adam cautioned.

Captain Thorath stepped closer to Adam. The commander appeared to be still puzzled over what to do next, what to say, 'You made an unusual wish with one of our stones,' he said finally.

'I wished for galactic peace,' Adam said.

'You did?' Fur said with interest.

'Yes,' Adam said with a sad note in his voice. He gestured to the warships, the armed robots that continued to point at them with their weapons. "But it doesn't look like my wish will be granted any time soon.'

'But it must be granted,' Fur said with excitement in his tone.

Captain Thorath quickly held up a scaly hand. 'We need not go into that right now,' he said.

Fur stepped forward. 'But you know the rules, Commander. The whole galaxy knows them.' Fur turned back to Adam. 'Tell me, was your wish on the same order as the others?'

'This is nonsense,' Teeh interrupted, speaking to

the warship commander. 'Let's kill them all now and eat their skins.'

'His wish was on the same order,' Sally said to Fur. 'The Collector stated that fact.'

Fur smiled and turned to Captain Thorath. 'Then you cannot collect on any of their wishes. Not until every wish on the order has been granted. Those are your own rules written by your own senate.'

'We don't grant the wishes until the debts have been paid off,' Teeh said bitterly.

Fur shook his head. 'Your commander knows better. You grant the wishes, then come to collect the debts, then give the stuff back when the debts have been paid off.' He added with bitterness, 'Of course you never really have to give anything away. All your slaves die before they get back what they wished for.'

'As well they should,' Teeh said. 'Do we look like we're stupid? We . . .'

'Shut up, Teeh,' Captain Thorath told the slave boss. He spoke to the gang. 'It is true what your trader friend says. We cannot legally collect on your debts until all the wishes on the same order have been fulfilled. But Adam, because your wish is so unusual, we doubt if we will ever be able to grant it.' He paused. 'For that reason we would prefer you make another wish. Something simple, easy to make in our factories.'

'But if I do that we will all end up as slaves,' Adam said.

Captain Thorath sighed. 'I was afraid you would say that.' He spread his hands. 'Then what should we do? I am open to suggestions.'

Fur spoke to the gang. 'Don't do anything. Let the wish for galactic peace remain. Then the Kaster will be obliged to fulfil it before they can come after you again. And that wish will never be granted, especially by the Kaster. They are always at war with somebody.'

'But we can't let these humans go!' Teeh broke in. 'This one here electrocuted my snout!'

'Good for her,' Captain Thorath muttered, thinking, his gaze momentarily far away. Finally he turned back to the gang. 'Very well, a rule is a rule, and we shouldn't be breaking our own if we expect others to listen to them.' He drew in a deep breath. 'You are not obliged to pay your debts until all the wishes on your order have been fulfilled.'

110

'Which in practice means you won't ever have to pay them,' Fur said.

'Do we get to keep the things we wished for?' Sally asked.

Captain Thorath hesitated, 'Yes.'

Sally squealed with delight. 'I knew what I was doing all along! I'm rich!'

But Captain Thorath pointed at Fur and Hironee. 'But this trader is coming back to Tallas 4 with me, to be tried and executed. And Teeh, you can do what you wish with this disobedient slave.'

'I will eat her flesh in front of her eyes!' Teeh exclaimed.

Hironee cowered. 'No.'

'Get over the flesh thing already,' Sally muttered. She put her arm around Hironee's shoulders and spoke to the commander. 'You can't hurt our friend. We won't let you.'

Fur looked anxiously around. 'Why isn't anyone hugging me?'

Teeh gloated at Sally. 'We can do whatever we want with both of them.'

Adam took another step forward. 'Wait a second. Captain Thorath, between the four of us we wished for some pretty expensive items. We got money, a laser pistol, a force field generator, a new telescope, spring outfits. These things must have cost the Kaster a pretty penny.'

Captain Thorath studied him. 'What is your point, young man?'

'What if we give you these things back?' Adam said. 'And in exchange you let Hironee and Fur go?'

Sally took her arm of Hironee. 'Don't give my money back,' Sally whispered to Adam.

'I really like that telescope,' Watch said.

'Your proposition is an interesting one,' Captain Thorath said. 'A dead trader is of little use to us, and I am sure Teeh here has plenty of slaves to eat.' He paused. 'I will accept your offer to return all the goods, as long as you can all agree on the offer.'

'I agree,' Fur said.

'You don't count,' Sally snapped at him. 'I say we return everything except the money and Hironee gets to go free with us.'

'But Fur is our friend,' Adam protested.

'But we haven't known him that long,' Watch said.

Adam held up his hands. 'Wait a second! How

can we have galactic peace if we can't even have peace among ourselves? We're all friends here. We have to stick together like friends should. We either return everything and all go free or else we remain here and labour away until the end of our lives.' He paused for effect. 'What's it going to be?'

Watch shrugged. 'I already have a pretty good telescope at home.'

Sally hesitated. 'I suppose I will get rich anyway, either as a famous actress or a best-selling novelist.'

Adam smiled and offered his hand to Captain Thorath. 'It's a deal.'

Captain Thorath shook his hand and nodded. 'You continue to think big, Adam. The galaxy needs more people like you.'

Hironee turned to Sally. 'I get to return to Zanath?'

Sally hugged her. 'Yeah, and your ticket's costing me a couple of million. But don't let that bother you. I just mention it in passing.'

Fur beamed and puffed on his cigar. 'I can take you back to Zanath. Heck, I can take the rest of you back to Earth.' He turned towards his spaceship, and the rest of them followed. 'I've got to see this famous Spooksville. It sounds like a happening place.'

Sally glanced one last time at desolate Amacron 37 and turned up her nose.

'Yeah,' she said. 'At least it beats this place.'

Spooksville

The Secret Path

Adam has never met anyone like Sally before.

She tells him terrifying stories about what happens to kids in Spooksville. Adam doesn't believe her – would you?

Then he meets Watch who leads them along the Secret Path into Spooksville's other dimension.

A place where fear kills.

A place from which few return.

Spooksville

The Howling Ghost

Cindy's younger brother, Neil, had disappeared. She knows a ghost has abducted him, but nobody will believe her.

Nobody, that is, except Sally. Sally believes in ghosts, and she knows they are a dime a dozen in Spooksville. So, with Adam and Watch, she tries to rescue Neil.

But this is a nasty ghost. It hates *living* kids . . .

Spooksville

The Haunted Cave

There's a famous cave outside Spooksville. Adam, Sally, Watch and Cindy can't wait to explore it. But that's a big mistake.

The moment they enter the cave, the entrance closes behind them.

They're trapped in darkness.

Then they realise that something is following them. Something big, black and very hungry . . .

Spooksville

Aliens in the Sky

Bright lights in the sky can only mean one thing: UFOs!

When one of them lands by the reservoir, Adam and his friends are intrigued. But they're not so sure when the aliens emerge from the spaceship. And especially not when the aliens insist they accompany them on to the UFO.

Then the UFO takes off. And it doesn't look like the aliens will be bringing them back home . . .

Spooksville
CHRISTOPHER PIKE

❏	66113 5	The Secret Path	£2.99
❏	66114 3	The Howling Ghost	£2.99
❏	66115 1	The Haunted Cave	£2.99
❏	66116 X	Aliens in the Sky	£2.99
❏	66117 8	The Cold People	£2.99

*All Hodder Children's books are available at your local bookshop or newsagent,
or can be ordered direct from the publisher. Just tick the titles you want and fill in
the form below. Prices and availability subject to change without notice.*

Hodder Children's Books, Cash Sales Department, Bookpoint, 39 Milton
Park, Abingdon, OXON, OX14 4TD, UK. If you have a credit card you may
order by telephone – (01235) 831700.

Please enclose a cheque or postal order made payable to Bookpoint Ltd to
the value of the cover price and allow the following for postage and packing:
UK & BFPO – £1.00 for the first book, 50p for the second book, and 30p
for each additional book ordered up to a maximum charge of £3.00.
OVERSEAS & EIRE – £2.00 for the first book, £1.00 for the second book,
and 50p for each additional book.

Name ....

Address ....

....

....

If you would prefer to pay by credit card, please complete:
Please debit my Visa/Access/Diner's Card/American Express (delete as
applicable) card no:

Signature ....

ExpiryDate ....

More young spine-tinglers from Hodder Children's Books
Laugh till you scream with
Tom B. Stone's
GRAVEYARD SCHOOL series

❑	63693 9	Deadly Dinners	£2.99
❑	63684 7	The Headless Bike Rider	£2.99
❑	63600 9	Wicked Wheels	£2.99
❑	63601 7	Little Pet Werewolf	£2.99
❑	63602 5	Revenge of the Dinosaurs	£2.99
❑	63603 3	Camp Dracula	£2.99
❑	66476 2	Slime Lake	£2.99

All Hodder Children's books are available at your local bookshop or newsagent, or can be ordered direct from the publisher. Just tick the titles you want and fill in the form below. Prices and availability subject to change without notice.

Hodder Children's Books, Cash Sales Department, Bookpoint, 39 Milton Park, Abingdon, OXON, OX14 4TD, UK. If you have a credit card you may order by telephone – (01235) 831700.

Please enclose a cheque or postal order made payable to Bookpoint Ltd to the value of the cover price and allow the following for postage and packing:
UK & BFPO – £1.00 for the first book, 50p for the second book, and 30p for each additional book ordered up to a maximum charge of £3.00.
OVERSEAS & EIRE – £2.00 for the first book, £1.00 for the second book, and 50p for each additional book.

Name ....

Address ....

....

....
If you would prefer to pay by credit card, please complete:
Please debit my Visa/Access/Diner's Card/American Express (delete as applicable) card no:

Signature ....

ExpiryDate ....